BOO!

For Jessie (and Leo and Rosie) R.A.
For Sarah and Allie, we know how this feels, A.G.

With thanks to Judith Brinsford – R.A.

First published in hardback in Great Britain by HarperCollins Publishers Ltd in 2003
First published in paperback by HarperCollins Children's Books in 2004
This edition published by HarperCollins Children's Books in 2006

1 3 5 7 9 10 8 6 4 2

ISBN-13: 978-0-00-722468-5
ISBN-10: 0-00-722468-0

HarperCollins Children's Books is a division of HarperCollins Publishers Ltd.

Visit our website at: www.harpercollinschildrensbooks.co.uk

Printed and bound by Printing Express, Hong Kong

BOO!

Ros Asquith

Illustrated by Andi Good

HarperCollins *Children's Books*

My mum said to me today,
"You silly little moose!
You're so shy,
You wouldn't say,
'BOO!' to a goose."

"Well," I thought, "I could...
If I saw a goose, I would."

Instead...

I saw a **monster**
But it didn't see me.

I crept up right behind it,
And shouted, noisily...

But the monster wasn't frightened.
It didn't seem to care.
It just danced around in circles,
As if I wasn't there.

Then I found a
tiger –

Or I thought I had,
at least –

It was very, very scary,
As I might have been his tea,
But the tiger wasn't fierce at all –
He came and purred at me.

Soon I saw a great big **bear**
But he didn't frighten me!
I stood quite still in front of him
And yelled, **ferociously...**

But the bear hardly noticed me –
He showed no sign of fear.
So I gave him a cuddle
And he grinned from ear to ear.

Next I met some pirates
With flags and chains and knives.
I thought, "I'll make these pirates
All run for their lives!"

I really scared those pirates!
They vanished right away!
Shame –
I would have liked it
If a pirate came to play.

So when I saw some **cowboys**
Galloping away,
I didn't say "**BOO!**" – I said,
"Please stay! Can I play?"

But they said,

"GO AWAY!"

"Don't be sad," my mum told me,
"You've been so brave today.
The cowboys didn't mean it.
They're asking you to play.

Now you deserve a small surprise.
Guess what I have for you?"
I hoped that it would be a goose
So I could call him...

BOO!

Collect them all – while stocks last!

ISBN: 0-00-722471-0

The zebra who trots into trouble

BRIAN PATERSON

ZIGBY
CAMPS OUT

ISBN: 0-00-722472-9

Michael Rosen & Jonathan Langley

A noisy night

Snore!

Joe a dozy Dog

ISBN: 0-00-722469-9

illustrated by Michael Dicks

written by Tony

Oscar
and Hoo

ISBN: 0-00-722464-8

Jonathan Emmett
& Curtis Jobling

DINOSAURS
AFTER DARK

ISBN: 0-00-722465-6

JANE YOLEN & MARK TEAGUE

How Do
Dinosaurs
Say Good
Night?

ISBN: 0-00-722467-2

James Sage & Russell Ayto

Fat Cat

ISBN: 0-00-722466-4

Mandy Stanley

The Dancing Rabbit

Lettice

ISBN: 0-00-722468-0

Ros Asquith & Andi Good

BOO!

ISBN: 0-007224470-2

Andy Cutbill

A small boy in a world with no words

Albie
and the
Space Rocket

HarperCollins Children's Books